The Land of Starry Night

Robin Helm

Illustrated by Gail Lyster

© 2011 by Robin Helm.
Illustrations by Gail Lyster.
All rights reserved.

Printed in the United States of America

ISBN 978-1463717421

www.TheLandofStarryNight.com

Produced in association with
Keokee Publishing
P.O. Box 722
Sandpoint, ID 83864
(208) 263-3573

For the child in each of us.

I'd scramble up a moonbeam,
I'd climb and climb and climb,
Then join the Starry Children
Sitting down at suppertime.

You see . . .
  the twinkling dots of white
Which speckle nighttime skies,
Are Starry Boys and Starry Girls
In necklaces of fireflies.

All night long we'd run and play
Wild games of hide—and—seek.
We'd splash in puddles and we'd feed
The Starfish in the creek.

Tag and leap frog,
 hopscotch too—
We'd jump
 and laugh
 and sing.
And at the park
 in Starry Night
We'd spin
 and slide
 and swing.

Or sometimes when we'd sleepy grow
We'd watch the world go round,
And ponder war and peace and love,
And matters less profound.

And sometimes on those starry nights,
I'd tell the children tales
Of dogs and kittens I have loved,
Of elephants and whales.

I'd tell the Starry Children
what it's like to climb a tree,

Just how to build a birdhouse,
And why it's fun to ski.

I'd speak to them of rainbows and
of eagles soaring by.
I'd talk about my garden where
orange poppies grow knee high.

"But here," the Starry Children said,
"We've fireflies for friends,
And meals of milk and cookies,
And playtime never ends."

"We sleep on cloud-filled pillows, and
We Children don't grow old.
We're never ever hungry and
We're never ever cold."

"There's never any loneliness
Or sadness here, or fear.
Plus . . . we celebrate our birthdays
Twelve or thirteen times a year!"

"Please . . .
　we'll share with you our trains and trucks,
Our dolls and balls and toys.
So please, oh, please stay here with us—
Us Starry Girls and Boys."

Woefully I looked at them
And very softly said,
"But what about the colors
Of blue and green and red?"

"In Land of Starry Night there's just
A deep, dark black— and white;
No sunset hues of lavender
As day gives way to night;"

"No red balloons,
  no green green grass,
No yellow butterflies,
And worst of all, no rainbows
Ever arch above your skies."

"Up here I'd miss the sounds of Earth—
Of waves upon the shore,
Of birdsong and soft breezes through
My oaks and sycamore."

"I'd miss my pink nosed puppy and
Our daily morning run.
Who'd weed my bed of flowers—
Poppies sprouting in the sun?"

"Sun . . .
I need to bathe in sunshine as
It dances on the lake.
I want to smell the roses
   through
My window as I wake."

"And while my world's imperfect with
its sadness, storms, and strife—
The Earth is home, and home is where
I want to live my life."

So . . .
I hugged the Starry Children, each
Aglow with fireflies.
I tried to hold my tears back as
I whispered my goodbyes.

Then...
I slithered down a moonbeam to
My house and trees and pet.
And though I miss the Children,
  still,
I haven't gone back yet.

On sunny days I'm certain that
The choice I made was right.
But . . .
I'll always love the Children of
The Land of Starry Night.

I will ALWAYS love the Children of
The Land of Starry Night.

Robin Eresman Helm, M.D. grew up in New England. Some of her most peaceful childhood moments were spent perched in a hemlock tree surveying the fields and river down the hill to the west. College, medical school, and residency training carried her ever farther westward. Today she practices pediatrics in Sandpoint, Idaho and lives in a little cabin on the shore of Lake Pend Oreille with her husband, dog, and cat. On clear nights, a full moon rising over the mountains to the east casts a silvery swath of light upon the water—a swath so dense as to form a path leading upward into the starry heavens. It leads, she is certain, to The Land of Starry Night.

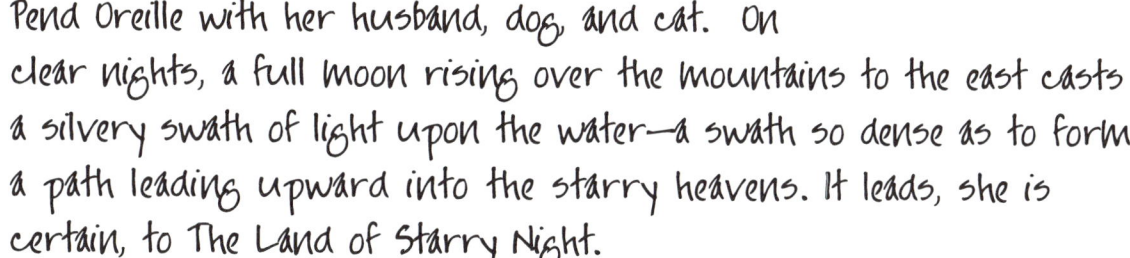

Sandpoint artist Gail Wolters Lyster has embraced a variety of mediums over the years, from leather and native materials to oils and watercolors. She is perhaps best known for her brilliantly colored glazed ceramic tiles. Pencil and layered watercolors were used to illustrate The Land of Starry Night. Earth's softly hued mountains, lake, and trees were inspired by images of her beloved north Idaho. Join Gail Lyster on beautiful Planet Earth as well as in the whimsical, magical world of Starry Night.

Made in the USA
Charleston, SC
23 August 2011